Onyx Kids

Shiloh's School Dayz

Book Five

The Secret Admirer

By Rita Onyx

Onyx Star Publishing, LLC
Delaware, USA

Publisher's Note: This is a work of fiction. Names, characters, places, and incidents are either the product of the author's imagination or are used fictitiously, and any resemblance to actual persons, living or dead, business establishments, events, or locales are entirely coincidental.

Copyright © 2019 by Rita Onyx

Published by Onyx Star Publishing, LLC
Delaware.
http://www.onyxstarpublishing.com/

For publishing and distribution inquiries contact:
contact@onyxstarpublishing.com

Printed in the United States of America

Cover art by Sinead Onyx
Illustrations by Shalom Onyx

Onyx Kids is a trademark of Onyx Star Media LLC

All rights reserved. In accordance with the U.S. Copyright Act of 1976, the scanning, uploading, and electronic sharing of any part of this book without the permission of the publisher constitute unlawful piracy and theft of the author's intellectual property. No part of this book may be reproduced or transmitted in any form or by any means, electronic or mechanical, including photocopying, recording, or by any information storage and retrieval system, without the written permission from the publisher, except in the case of brief quotations embodied in critical articles or reviews.

Table of Contents

Chapter One

Love Isn't Logical

It was mid-morning on an ordinary Tuesday at Cornerstone Middle School. Shiloh hadn't seen his best friend Evan for almost a week. Evan was home sick with a bad cold since the third week of January. Lots of kids seemed to get sick after the excitement of the holidays, but it was rare to be out for so long. School seemed strange to Shiloh without Evan being around. Everyone was bustling about, but somehow the halls seemed empty and Shiloh's brain seemed glazed over. Nothing seemed different or fascinating. Shiloh could almost predict what everyone would say or do.

One day at recess, instead of going outdoors into the icy winter air to shoot some hoops, Shiloh decided to go down into Evan's secret lab. The secret lab was hidden down in the abandoned basement of the school.

Evan had set it up the previous summer when he was in summer school. He and Evan and their friend Desirae were the only ones who went down to the lab on a regular basis. Another friend of theirs, Roxy, had been down there once, but she couldn't take the vinegary smell from Evan's biology experiments so she hadn't come back. Even the teachers and the principal didn't know about it. The three friends were hoping to keep it that way.

During the Christmas season, Shiloh, Evan and Desirae had decorated the lab and it had become Secret Santa's workshop. Between the three of them they had fixed so many broken and unwanted toys and made them like new. They were able to give away hundreds of toys to needy kids. The three of them had loved every minute of it, but after the holiday was over they thought it was best to shut down the colorful indoor lights. They didn't want the school's electric bill to become so high that someone started asking questions, especially if that someone was Ms. Sufferin.

Shiloh wandered down to the basement, making sure that no one was following him. When he got to the end of the empty hallway, he pushed open the heavy door and went down the winding staircase. The door used to say, "Staff only," but the "S" was worn off and so was the cross mark on the "t." It made it seem like the sign said "laff only." Even though Shiloh had seen this door a thousand times, it always made him smile.

The stairs creaked under his feet as he pushed open the door to the secret lab. The lab seemed stuffy. Evan hadn't been there for over a week and some of the cobwebs hanging from the ceiling lights had gotten quite large. For a few seconds, Shiloh thought about getting a broom and cleaning up, but then he thought about what would happen if he disturbed any spiders.

Nope, he thought. He was going to leave them alone.

Instead, he sat on one of the metal stools and took out his phone. He sent a text to Evan.

Hey, Evan. Are you feeling any better? Are you really sick or are you just catching up on Netflix?

Normally, Evan wrote back within a few seconds, but there was no reply. Then, Shiloh heard a noise in the hallway.

Oh no! He thought to himself. *Who could that be? I hope it's not one of the teachers or the janitors.* The footsteps got closer and closer to the door. He went by the door and hid. If whoever it was opened the door he would be hidden behind it.

The door opened slightly and then Shiloh saw Desirae peek inside. She turned and looked and saw Shiloh staring at her. She yelped in surprise.

"Shiloh, you scared me! What are you doing in here?!" Desirae asked as she walked in.

"I'm so glad it's you. I was afraid one of the teachers had followed me," he was so relieved. "I was bored so I came down here. What are you doing here?"

"Same," said Desirae. She twirled around aimlessly and then she reached up and pulled down one of the huge cobwebs hanging from the ceiling lights. "It looks as if the spiders have taken over."

"I thought about cleaning up a bit, but uh, recess is going to be over soon," said Shiloh. He wasn't going to admit that he didn't want to deal with spiders to Desirae. "I just texted Evan a while ago and he didn't write back. That isn't like him. I'm kind of worried."

"Why don't we stay after school one day and clean it up so it won't be a so much of a mess when Evan gets back," said Desirae.

"How about Thursday or Friday?" Shiloh asked.

"That works for me," said Desirae.

Just then Shiloh's phone pinged. Evan had finally written back.

> I'm not doing so
> hot. Actually,
> that's not the best
> way to say it
> because I am hot. I
> still have a fever
> and my head feels
> like it has chewing
> gum wadded up in
> it. It's probably
> going to be a few
> more days before I
> can come back.
> I don't want to
> give anyone at
> school my germs!

Shiloh showed Desirae the message. "I feel so bad that he's sick."

"Me too," said Shiloh. He texted back.

```
Do you want
anything after
school?
```

"I guess we better head back," said
Shiloh. "Mrs. Dominguez's art class
is next on our agenda."

They closed the door to the secret
lab, went up the winding staircase,
and through the heavy door. No one
was in the hallway. They stopped for
a second as another ping came in on
Shiloh's phone. Evan had written
back.

```
Thanks, but I don't
want you guys to
catch my germs
either. Besides, my
mom is feeding me
so much chicken
soup I feel like my
blood is now made
of broth. I'm just
going to binge
watch Star Trek and
Star Wars then go
on forums and troll
their superfans by
telling them that
the real G.O.A.T.
is Doctor. Who.
```

"Only Evan would think of Doctor. Who," said Desirae as she laughed.

Shiloh rolled his eyes. "He's not even British so I don't know why he's such a huge fan."

"You don't have to be British to like that show."

"I know, but I never heard of it until he made me watch hours of it last year when he discovered it."

"Maybe one day you can show it to me so I can get caught up. Just a thought," Desirae said casually as she walked ahead.

Shiloh paused for a second at her statement. Evan had a huge crush on Desirae, but he wasn't sure if she knew about it or not. This was getting sticky...

Meanwhile at Evan's house, Evan was having a pity party. *I can't believe I can't get rid of this cold,* he thought to himself. *I'm going to be so behind on everything when I get back to school.*

He could smell the next batch of chicken soup that his mom was fixing for him and almost gagged. *I'm sick of chicken soup and I'm sick of this cold and I'm just...sick of being sick!* It was nice of Desirae and Shiloh to be in touch, but he wasn't too happy that they were down in the secret lab together without him. *I know Desirae likes Shiloh. I just hope she likes him as a friend and not a boyfriend,* Evan thought to himself. The idea that Desirae could like Shiloh better than she liked him wasn't helping Evan feel better. He moaned slightly and threw his head back deeper into his pillow.

His mom came in with the chicken soup on a tray and set it down on his desk.

"Are you feeling any better, honey?" his mom asked.

"Yes and no," Evan said. "My nose is less clogged, but I still feel like I have a fever."

His mom put her hand on his forehead. "Yeah, you're still a bit hot. I can give you some more aspirin in a little while."

"Do you think I could have something else besides chicken soup? Anything else?" he almost begged.

"You don't want my soup? Sweetie, it is full and rich with chicken stock, aromatic spices, and chunks of veggies. The steam from the soup will also help you breathe easier."

Evan just stared blankly. "So...can I have pizza?"

"Sure, you can have pizza, just close your eyes and pretend it's pizza."

"Mom, that's not the same!"

"Well, it's as close as you're going to get to pizza until you're over this cold. Now drink up," she said matter-of-factly.

"Mom, can I ask you something?"

"If it's about pizza or any other junk food, then no."

"No, it's about something else. I'll ask again for pizza later," Evan said, not noticing the look of exasperation on his mom's face at his last statement.

"What is it?" his mom asked.

"Why did you fall in love with Dad?"

"Oh boy, who is it? What's going on? Do you have a crush?" His mom was wide-eyed with interest.

"Never mind," Evan said as he turned on his iPad to start binge-watching. He was so embarrassed. He was close with his mom but he didn't want to talk about Desirae yet, especially since he thought she liked Shiloh.

His mom sat down in a chair next to Evan's bed. "Well, I know you'll tell me eventually. But as for me and your dad, you know that story, Evan. Your dad and I met in college. We were in a chemistry class together and the professor assigned us a joint project," said his mom. She brushed her hair back behind one ear and looked into the distance as she was thinking back on her college days.

"I know all that part," said Evan. "I just want to know specifically why you fell in love with him and not some other guy in the class."

"Well, it's not science you know. Falling in love with someone isn't logical. In fact, love isn't logical at all," his mom said. She seemed lost in thought.

"That's too bad," said Evan. "I wish it were more like science."

"Is there a girl you like at school?" his mom asked again.

"Yes, but I don't want to say who it is yet. All I will say is that she's really special. She's smart, funny, and cute too," said Evan in between coughing.

His mom smiled. "Back to your original question, I didn't really notice your dad that much until we started to work together. I had a boyfriend at the time so I wasn't really looking for love."

"Wow! I didn't know you had another boyfriend before Dad," Evan was surprised.

"There are a lot of things that kids don't know about their parents," said his mom. "Your dad was and is very smart and of course I found that attractive."

"Did you think he was nice-looking?" Evan asked.

"Yes, I did, in a cute sort of way, not movie-star handsome."

Evan groaned. "I heard that before. Girls always say "cute" when they're friend-zoning."

"No, that's not true! Well...I guess...sometimes," she admitted.

"What made it go from friend-zone to more?" Evan asked.

"Well, I do remember one day in particular. Your dad was going on and on about how we should set up the science project. I listened very carefully and then nodded my head, but then I told him that I thought I had an idea that might work better," she said.

"What happened?" Evan asked.

"Your dad sat down and didn't interrupt me for a full twenty minutes as I was explaining what I was thinking. He actually grabbed a pad of paper and took some notes."

"Was he frustrated?"

"Not at all. He seemed to be hanging on to every word I said."

"What did he say when you finished talking?" Evan asked. He had propped himself up in bed.

"I don't remember exactly what he said. He asked me a bunch of questions about the plan I had. They were really well-thought-out questions so I knew he'd been listening to me. Then, he nodded thoughtfully and said that he thought I was right. It was a better plan than the one he'd thought of, so we should follow my plan. He stood up, looked at me directly in the eyes and said something like—*Are you always this smart and this pretty*? And that was it."

"So, did you stop seeing your other boyfriend?" Evan asked.

"Not right away. Your dad was kind of shy and it took him almost two months after that to ask me out on a date," Evan's mom said.

"He didn't seem shy with what he said."

"I know, but I think he got cold feet right after," she laughed. Evan also laughed at the thought.

"Where did he take you on your first date?" Evan asked. He was taking mental notes in case Desirae ever said yes to a date with him.

"He took me to the planetarium. It was a very unusual place to go for a first date, but I loved it!" she said. "Okay, that's enough talk for now. I want this bowl empty and then I want you to get some sleep. We can talk later about this girl you like. That is, if you want to."

"Sure," said Evan as he slurped up his soup. He drank it in a few minutes and then he was out like a light.

Chapter Two

Cornerstone's Valentine's Day Dance

It was Wednesday morning and Shiloh had managed to get to homeroom on time for once. He was almost always late. The ironic thing was that when he slipped into his seat, Ms. Sufferin wasn't paying any attention. She was out in the hallway chatting it up with Mr. Thomas, their English teacher. For the life of him, Shiloh couldn't understand what Mr. Thomas saw in her. Ms. Sufferin was strict and humorless or at least she seemed that way around the students. Mr. Thomas was her exact opposite. He was easy-going and friendly.

The students respected Mr. Thomas, but they feared Ms. Sufferin or Suffering as they called her behind her back. She used her pointer like a lethal weapon and never gave an inch when it came to class rules and regulations. From the very first day of school, she had seemed to be on

Shiloh's case. He'd never had a teacher dislike him so much. Sufferin seemed to think he was some kind of troublemaker just because he laughed at what he thought was a joke she made on the first day of class.

Seeing that she was occupied, Shiloh decided to take a chance and send a text to Evan. He used "the raven" as his code for Ms. Sufferin since she almost always wore stark black clothes to class. Because of the fact that Mr. Thomas was linked to Ms. Sufferin, Shiloh nicknamed him "Edgar Allan Poe" after Poe's famous poem, "The Raven." He used the code EAP for short. He and Evan frequently used these kinds of codes so that if the teachers took their phones they would have no idea what they had been talking about.

> Are you feeling any
> better? The Raven
> is out talking with
> EAP in the hallway
> again. For once,
> I'm early and
> she didn't even
> notice.

Now that Evan was starting to recuperate, his texts had started to come in a bit faster, but not at the lightning speed Shiloh was used to. He wrote back in a few minutes.

> You can't win with the raven. I'm starting to feel better. I hope I'll be back at school on Monday.
> I'm only coughing a little.

Shiloh breathed a sigh of relief. He couldn't wait for his best friend to come back.

Valerie Collins was sitting next to Shiloh in class. He had spoken to her a few other times, but they didn't know each other well. She touched his arm to get his attention.

"Hey, Shiloh, do you have a pencil I could borrow?" Valerie asked. "I was going to put a couple of new ones in my backpack this morning, but I forgot."

"Sure," said Shiloh. He quickly found a couple of extra pencils and handed them to her. He noticed that she smiled shyly at Shiloh and he smiled back, but they couldn't talk anymore because at that moment the pounding of heels signaled that Ms. Sufferin was headed back to the classroom.

She walked in, grabbed her pointer, and started to walk around the room looking for infractions, just as if she were a sergeant and the students were soldiers in the military. Shiloh had quickly pulled his legs under his desk. She was forever hitting the side of his boots with her pointer. It was true that Shiloh was growing like a weed and he could barely fit into the student desks. He was hoping that when he got to seventh grade the following year, the desks were going to be larger.

Some students were criticized for
not hanging their winter jackets up
on the rack. For some reason,
Sufferin hated it when they slung
their jackets over the backs of their
chairs. She walked all around the
classroom before she came back to
the front and gave a sideways glance
at Shiloh. She seemed to be upset
that she couldn't find anything
wrong with him. His feet weren't in
the aisle and he had remembered to
hang his jacket up too.

Even though she couldn't find
anything wrong, she decided to use
his past errors to make a statement.
"Well isn't it a pleasant surprise to
see that your huge clodhoppers

aren't sticking out in the aisle for once and that your jacket is hung up properly. Are you trying to impress me?" Sufferin asked. The class was already quiet, but now they went totally silent.

Shiloh had no clue how to respond, but before he could even form any words, Ms. Sufferin continued, "I guess the cat has got your tongue." Shiloh decided not to answer her and prolong her attention on him any longer than necessary. He was wondering what Desirae was thinking. She was sitting in the back of the class so he couldn't see her face.

Ms. Sufferin pivoted on her heels and went to stand behind her desk. "Good morning, students. As you know the plans for the new gym are well underway. Unfortunately, it's still way too cold for the construction team to break ground so it might be this time next year before it's finally built." There was an audible sigh from the class although they were careful not to be too loud because Ms. Sufferin didn't allow it.

"I know you're disappointed that you won't have a new gym to ruin as soon as possible, but I do have some other news to report," Ms. Sufferin continued. "This year Cornerstone has decided to have an after-school Valentine's Day dance. I don't have all the details but I'm sure you're going to ask me a million questions anyway."

Desirae immediately raised her hand. "Yes, Desirae, what's your question?" Ms. Sufferin asked.

"Do we have to have a date to go to the dance?" Desirae asked. A few of the girls in the back of the class were whispering as quietly as they could.

"Of course not. This isn't the 18th century. You can go alone or with friends or with your cat. I don't care," she scowled, but then her face softened a bit. "That being said, if you want to attend the dance with someone special and save all your dances for that person I don't think

27

it would be a problem," said Ms. Sufferin as she glanced dreamily over in the direction of Mr. Thomas's class. Shiloh cringed.

Valerie raised her hand, "Ms. Sufferin, will the boys be required to go?"

Quiet giggling traveled through the class from row to row. Her scowl returned.

"No, but the teachers and principal are all aware of the fact that middle-school boys aren't as interested in the dance as the girls are. However, since the principal thinks that dancing is a fun social skill, we will be giving away prizes during the evening and offering extra credit to those who come to the dance so we hope that will be enough incentive for the boys to attend," said Ms. Sufferin as she glared at Shiloh.

One of the boys in the front of the class raised his hand. "Yes, Trey, what is your question?" Ms. Sufferin asked.

"Will the boys have to wear a suit and a tie?" Trey asked. He sounded almost scared.

"I don't understand why you would ask that question. Would you like to wear your PJs? Or how about your shirts and jeans that have holes in them which you all think is fashion." She narrowed her eyes at him and paused for a second.

"Of course you have to wear a suit and tie! You will be required to wear the proper attire," said Ms. Sufferin. "I will be handing out a sheet tomorrow that provides rules for what is acceptable and what's not. I do know my labels you know," she sniffed. "That sheet will also give the start and end times for the dance. The prizes and rules for getting extra-credit will be listed as well. There's going to be a lot of tacky decorations and horrible music so get ready to have lots of fun," she ended flatly.

Desirae raised her hand again. "Yes, Desirae, why do you have another question? I mean, yes tell me your question?" Ms. Sufferin pasted her normal grimace which she thought was a smile.

"What type of dancing will we be doing, Ms. Sufferin?" Desirae asked.

"I will have a list for that as well. Everyone will be on their best behavior. I am taking my ruler and trust me I will be using it to make sure everyone is a good distance from each other. That's enough for today. We have to move on," said Ms. Sufferin.

Shiloh was thinking, *leave it to Sufferin to take the joy out of something that should be fun,* but he was trying not to let it show on his face.

It was hard for the students to concentrate on the other announcements. All they were thinking about was the dance and whether they wanted to go or not. They tried hard to stay still in their seats so Ms. Sufferin wouldn't notice that they couldn't concentrate.

After homeroom was over, Valerie walked out near Shiloh. "Shiloh, are you going to go to the dance?" she asked him shyly.

"I'll probably go," Shiloh shrugged. "I can't wait to enjoy the *tacky decorations and horrible music*," he said in his best Ms. Sufferin voice.

Shiloh's imitation made Valerie laugh. "Do you know how to dance?" she asked.

"Not really, but I can fake it as well as anyone else," said Shiloh with a grin.

"Will you...will you...save a dance for me?" she asked.

Shiloh almost missed what she said with the hustle and bustle going on in the hallway. "Sure," said Shiloh. He felt a little awkward because he hadn't known that Valerie liked him at all. They had only talked a few times under the watchful eye of Sufferin.

As they got near the lockers, Valerie waved goodbye and then Shiloh heard Desirae coming up next to him. "Hey, Shiloh, have you heard from Evan?" Desirae asked.

"Yep. He thinks he'll be back by Monday," said Shiloh as he took his huge science textbook out of his locker.

"Oh, that's a long time," said Desirae, "I hope he's doing better."

"I'm probably going to drop by his house tonight and see how he's doing. Do you want me to tell him anything?" asked Shiloh.

"Can you give him a note for me?" Desirae asked.

"Sure," said Shiloh.

"Okay, great. I don't have it written up yet. I'll give it to you later today in art class," she said. "I gotta go to math class now. My head is spinning with algebra. Funny thing is, my mom told me that she didn't learn any algebra until high school."

"Good luck," said Shiloh.

"Thanks," said Desirae. "I'm gonna need it."

"I doubt it," said Shiloh. "You're good at science and math just like Evan." Desirae smiled at him, but she didn't say anything.

As she turned to walk away, Shiloh thought, *I wonder if Evan will be mad if I ask Desirae to dance with me.*

Suddenly, Desirae turned on her heel and ran up to Shiloh. She was so close that Shiloh could smell the strawberry scent in her hair. "I forgot to ask you which day you want to meet at the secret lab after school," she whispered.

"How does Thursday sound," said Shiloh.

"Works for me," said Desirae. "Talk with you later." Then, she turned and walked away leaving a hint of strawberries in the air.

Chapter 3

The Chemistry of Love

Shiloh got to science class in the nick of time. He really liked Mrs. Engelstrom and it was also fun because two of his other friends, Max and Roxy, were in the same class as well. Roxy was funny and smart and sometimes Shiloh got butterfly feelings around her too. Shiloh thought middle school was so hard to navigate sometimes with all of these feelings.

Before class, Mrs. Engelstrom pulled Shiloh aside to talk with him. She knew that Shiloh and Evan were best friends.

"Have you heard from Evan?" Mrs. Engelstrom asked. She seemed very concerned. "He's been out of school a long time."

"I got a text from him today. He says he thinks he'll be back at school on

Monday. He's had a really bad cold," said Shiloh.

"Well, we miss him around here," said Mrs. Engelstrom. "His science class depends on him to keep things exciting and I do too. He always makes me think."

"He definitely knows his stuff," Shiloh agreed.

Once everyone was settled in their seats, Mrs. Engelstrom started the class. "Today we're going to talk about biology and chemistry. Since it's going to be Valentine's Day soon, I thought we would talk about the biological and chemical changes that affect you when you're infatuated with someone or you think you're in love."

The students shifted in their seats. This was a topic they weren't expecting. It made quite a few of them a little uncomfortable. Mrs. Engelstrom felt their discomfort so she started to tell them a personal story to help them relax.

"I know it's hard for all of you to believe that I was your age once, but when I was in Middle School I had a huge crush on this boy in my class," she said. "Whenever I saw him, my knees kind of went weak. The funny part is that I never talked to him." Then, she walked up to the board and wrote *weak knees*.

"Does anyone else have a *love symptom* they're willing to share?" Mrs. Engelstrom asked.

The class was quiet for half a minute. Most of the students were too embarrassed to speak up. Then, Roxy raised her hand. "Yes, Roxy," said Mrs. Engelstrom.

"When I like someone that way I feel tongue-tied," Roxy said.

"Definitely," said Mrs. Engelstrom. "That's a good one. The words don't come out the way you want them to."

Surprisingly, Max raised his hand next. "Max, I'm all ears," said Mrs. Engelstrom as she stood poised at the whiteboard to write what Max was saying. "It will be good to get a male perspective."

"I get butterflies in my stomach and feel kinda lightheaded," said Max. "Is that what you mean?" Max was normally a jokester, but he was serious for once and Shiloh wondered if Max had a crush on anyone he knew. He spent a lot of time with Roxy, maybe it was her. Shiloh was very curious.

"Yes, that's perfect. Thank you for being willing to share," said Mrs. Engelstrom.

Now that Roxy and Max had broken the ice, the other students in class quickly raised their hands.

Soon, Mrs. Engelstrom had a long list:

Weak knees
Tongue-tied
Butterflies in stomach
Light-headed

Flush in the face
Sweaty palms
Not hungry
Can't sleep
Scrambled brain
Forgetful or distracted
Feel insecure
Feelings of jealousy
Mood swings
Like their smell

Shiloh added the last one and he realized when he was saying it that he was thinking of Desirae's strawberry-scented hair. He didn't have any of the other symptoms though, especially the *not hungry*

symptom, because he was always hungry. The only person that gave him sweaty palms or that he was tongue-tied around was Ms. Sufferin and he certainly didn't have a crush on her!

After she had written all their responses, Mrs. Engelstrom just looked at the list and said, "falling in love doesn't sound too pleasant."

Then, Roxy said out loud without raising her hand, "yes, but it's a good kind of sickness."

That made everyone in the class laugh.

Then, Mrs. Engelstrom went up to the board and showed how the brain and body chemistry changes when a person feels infatuation for someone else or falls in love. After she walked through the science and showed several chemistry and anatomy diagrams, she asked the class if they had any questions.

Roxy quickly raised her hand. "Yes, Roxy, what is your question?" Mrs. Engelstrom asked.

"Is there any science that explains why you fall in love with someone in the first place?" she asked.

"Well, that's a good question and I'm sure many people would love to have the answer in the hopes that they could give someone a magic potion to fall in love with them," said Mrs. Engelstrom. "Science has some of the answers, but the truth is that when you fall in love with someone, logic and science take a back seat to the art of romance."

Max raised his hand. "Do people just fall in love once?"

"That's another good question. There have been surveys done to answer it. Some people only fall in love once, but the average number of times a person falls in love during their lifetime is four times. That's important to remember because the first person you fall in love with might not end up being your life-long partner," said Mrs. Engelstrom.

At this point, she realized that they had strayed far from the science lesson that she had planned to teach. However, she didn't feel bad about it. She knew that her students had lots of questions and since they were so interested in the topic she didn't want to stop the conversation.

When Mrs. Engelstrom's class was over, Shiloh found himself wandering aimlessly in the hallway. It was time for recess, but he didn't feel like going outdoors and he was too tired to wander down to the secret lab.

Roxy was hovering nearby trying to muster up the courage to talk to Shiloh. Although they were friends she was hoping for more. Just as she was about to go up to him, Desirae emerged from her math class and walked alongside Shiloh.

Roxy and Desirae were friends, but Roxy didn't think Desirae liked her that much. Roxy tried to get to know her but it seemed like Desirae, Shiloh, and Evan were the Three Musketeers and she felt like the outsider. That's why she spent more time with Max.

Why can't Desirae hang around Evan more? Doesn't she know he has a huge crush on her? Roxy mused. In fact, it seemed that everyone at Cornerstone knew that, with the possible exception of Desirae herself. The thing that she couldn't figure out was whether Shiloh had a crush on Desirae too.

Roxy watched every move Shiloh made in the classes they had

42

together. He was always friendly and pleasant to her, but other than that he had never shown any interest in trying to get to know her better. Roxy had told her mom all about her crush on Shiloh and her mom had tried to assure her that this was a part of growing up and not to get too anxious over it. But, even though she tried to listen to her mom's wise words, Roxy couldn't help being nervous around Shiloh.

She knew she wasn't alone in her romantic feelings for Shiloh. Lots of other girls seemed all fluttery around him too, but Shiloh didn't seem to notice. It made Roxy think that Shiloh was very self-confident and must have a happy family life. That made her like him even more, because it was something she lacked in her own life. Her mom had always been there for her, but her dad had left when Roxy was young and it was one of the reasons she never felt that self-assured.

As she saw Desirae and Shiloh happily talking, she gave up and decided to go outdoors and stand in the cold winter air for a few minutes.

Desirae and Shiloh had been chatting about whether there was anything they could do to make Evan feel better. "Here's the note I'd like you to give to Evan when you see him. I finished my work faster than I thought I would so I had time to write it," Desirae said as she handed a small pink envelope to Shiloh. "Are you sure you don't mind bringing it to him?"

"No, not at all," said Shiloh. "His house is right next door to mine." Shiloh looked down at the envelope that Desirae had handed him. For a second he was distracted. He was wondering what Desirae had written to Evan. It was a good thing that Desirae had sealed the envelope and put a cute flower sticker on it, otherwise Shiloh would have been tempted to open it and read it.

"It must be nice having him right next door," said Desirae. "I know you guys have been best friends for quite a while."

"Yeah, real nice," Shiloh said, unenthusiastically. *I wonder if she wishes she lived next door to him? Wait, why am I acting like this. He's my best friend. What's the matter with me? I need to chill.*

"I have an idea!" exclaimed Desirae. "Let's get Evan something special and put it down in the secret lab. Then, we can take a picture of the wrapped gift and send it to him on Friday. It might give him that extra boost to come back to school on Monday instead of feeling down over the weekend."

"That's a great idea, Desirae!" Shiloh said, trying to get back into a good mood. "I don't know what we could get for him, but I'll start thinking about it," said Shiloh.

"Wow! It's already three minutes before Mrs. Dominguez's art class. We better get going," said Desirae as she started to walk down the hallway.

"I didn't think I would like art class, but I really enjoy it," said Shiloh.

"I do too! Mrs. Dominguez is like a fireball of energy, but I find the class kind of relaxing," said Desirae.

"I think I feel about it the way that my mom feels about cooking and baking," said Shiloh. "I can always tell when she's anxious because she goes into the kitchen and bakes. She says it helps her to chill out."

"That's nice! You get all the goodies as a result," said Desirae. "My mom loves baking too."

The two friends walked side by side to Mrs. Dominguez's class.

Chapter Four

Gym Socks Aren't Romantic

Mrs. Dominguez was one of the newer teachers at Cornerstone, but Shiloh, Evan, and Desirae really liked her. She shared some things in common with Evan in that she was full of energy and vibrant. She was also always coming up with new ideas for the students to try. She taught them art techniques, but she also taught them about the history of art. The students were beginning to love all forms of art because of her mentoring.

There weren't assigned seats in her class and Shiloh, Desirae, and Evan usually sat together. All the teachers liked Evan so his absence from class was really obvious. In fact, when Desirae and Shiloh walked in, Mrs. Dominguez immediately noticed that Evan wasn't with them.

"Oh no!" she exclaimed as they walked in. "Another day without Mister Evan! He must be so sick!"

"He's getting better, Mrs. Dominguez," said Shiloh. "I'm going over to his house tonight. Is there anything you want me to tell him?"

"Yes! You tell him that he must get better very soon and that Mrs. Dominguez said so. All the teachers miss him! Cornerstone is not the same without our Mister Evan," she said.

"We miss him so much, Mrs. Dominguez. I hope he comes back before the Valentine's Day dance," said Desirae. Then, she blushed a little.

Her blush did not escape Shiloh's attention. *Chill Shiloh.* He said to himself.

Mrs. Dominguez looked very concerned, but she had a class full of students to teach so she turned her attention to starting the lesson.

The students got quiet, not because she demanded it like Ms. Sufferin, but because she always had something interesting to say.

"Class, today we are going to be working on some new projects!" exclaimed Mrs. Dominguez. "As all of you know, it will soon be Valentine's Day and we will be preparing decorations for the gymnasium to make it a little bit better than it is before the dance! And that isn't the only project we are going to be doing. We are going to create our own valentines as well. Remember, valentines can be given to anyone you love or like. You can even give one to your teacher if you like, hint, hint," she said. The class laughed.

Mrs. Dominguez paused for a second as she smiled and then she continued, "Before we begin, I want to tell you that Valentine's Day didn't start with hearts and flowers. Surprisingly, it started with a pagan holiday called Lupercalia that the Romans celebrated. But, by the 5th century, after Christianity was the official religion in Rome, the Pope decided to create a new holiday in honor of two Christian martyrs. Both of them were named Valentine. They had died for their faith on February 14. It wasn't until the Middle Ages that Valentine's Day became connected with romantic love. The Europeans thought that birds chose their mates and started their nesting season at that time. In the 1400s, people started to create romantic valentines for each other."

"Does anyone know when companies in the United States started to produce printed Valentine's Day cards?" Mrs. Dominguez asked.

The class was quiet because no one knew the answer. Mrs. Dominguez was thinking that if Evan had been there he might have known, but she didn't say anything to the students.

"It was in 1913," she said. "Over one hundred years ago! Since then people have been giving valentines that are already printed. However, that doesn't mean you can't create your own handmade valentine. That's what we're going to be doing in this class over the next week. And remember it doesn't have to be perfect. What's most important is that it's a true expression of your feelings of friendship or love."

Desirae was thinking about all the people she wanted to create valentines for. It was a long list. Shiloh was wondering whether Desirae's pink envelope held a valentine for Evan. If so, he knew that it would give Evan a huge boost. He had stuck it in a special pocket of his backpack so that he wouldn't forget to give it to Evan when he saw him later that night.

"But before we can start working on our own valentines, we need to finish the decorations for the gym," said Mrs. Dominguez. "For that we will actually need to work there because we'll be working on some huge canvases. So, pack up everything because we are going there now!"

The students began to buzz with excitement. It was always fun to get out of the classroom and work somewhere else. The gym was on the other side of the school so they would only have about half an hour to work once they got there, but this project was going to extend over several days.

"After today, we'll report there until Monday and then we'll come back to start our own valentines," said Mrs. Dominguez. "So, don't forget to arrive on time. If you forget and show up at our regular classroom, you'll be late. That gives us four class sessions to work on the decorations. Of course, my other classes will be working on them as well."

The students got into single file and started following Mrs. Dominguez down the hallway to get to the gym. The gym was connected to the rest of the school with a wide breezeway and when they got there the students fanned out and started talking with each other.

Mrs. Dominguez wasn't worried about the noise they were making until from the opposite direction

Ms. Sufferin began to walk toward them. As soon as she got close to Mrs. Dominguez she said, "Where are you taking all of them? To the circus?"

Mrs. Dominguez chose to ignore Ms. Sufferin's annoying sarcastic remark and said, "No, we are not going to the circus. We are going to the gymnasium to create art!"

Ms. Sufferin just looked down her nose at Mrs. Dominguez and sniffed, but she didn't say anything else.

Shiloh and Desirae were both on the other side of the breezeway and they snickered under their breaths. They hadn't realized that Ms. Sufferin was just as strict with some of the other teachers as she was with the students.

Ms. Sufferin just glared at all of them as she proceeded to walk through the breezeway with her harsh-sounding staccato heels.

When they got to the gym, it looked worse than usual. The floors looked like they hadn't been polished in a long time and it was quite cold even though the heat was running.

"This doesn't look like a very romantic setting," Desirae said to Shiloh.

"It's romantic if you like the smell of old gym socks," said Shiloh. He put his finger down his throat like he was going to puke.

Desirae laughed and then added, "the smell of old gym socks with a mix of sweat is NOT romantic at all!"

When they all got inside, Mrs. Dominguez put her hands on her hips. "It is a huge mess in here. We are going to have to do a lot of work to make this beautiful."
Shiloh and Desirae had already noticed that there were some huge canvases propped up with stands.

"Are we going to be working on those, Mrs. Dominguez?" Desirae asked as she pointed to the largest canvas.

"Yes!" exclaimed Mrs. Dominguez. "Everybody put on a painting smock. We are going to start with the background color today. It's all we have time to do. Shiloh, will you help me hand out the supplies."

"Sure," said Shiloh.

Shiloh helped Mrs. Dominguez as they handed out a bucket with water, a bucket of glaze, some cans of paint, and some sponges to every student. Mrs. Dominguez had set up everything for their use earlier in the day. She then quickly called out names. She had divided the class into eight groups with four students in each. Two groups would be assigned to each of the four canvases.

Desirae and Shiloh had been placed in a group with Mark and Audrey, two students they didn't know very well.

Mrs. Dominguez addressed the group, "Now we are going to use a technique called faux painting." She took a corner and quickly showed the students how to stroke the glaze on the canvas and then how to follow it with the paint. "The idea is to stroke paint on in a patterned way, but leave some of the white of the canvas to pop through. Then, you use these sponges to create an effect. If you do it properly, it will look like ancient walls in Italy or Spain or France. Audrey, you are one of our best artists. I want you to show the others how to draw roses, because I want hearts made of roses around the pairs of famous couples."

"I'll be glad to," said Audrey. She was proud that Mrs. Dominguez recognized her art talent.

"Oh! I love this!" exclaimed Desirae. "My mom and I have done some walls inside our house this way and they look so beautiful. Much better than the flat paint on the other walls. Shiloh, you're going to have to do the top of the canvas. I think you're the only one of us who's tall enough to reach."

"I'm afraid if I start, the paint will drip down on top of your heads," said Shiloh.

"Let's ask Mrs. Dominguez," said Audrey. Shiloh noticed that Audrey was cute and perky. She seemed added positive energy into their group and Shiloh liked that.

"Mrs. Dominguez, Shiloh's the tallest one in our group. If he paints the top of the canvas all the way across first will that work? He's afraid he's going to splatter us with paint," Audrey said.

"Thank you for reminding me, Audrey! I had completely forgotten that I had plastic headgear for all of you," said Mrs. Dominguez. She went rushing to the supply stand and handed out disposable plastic rain hats to all of them.

"I look weird in this," said Mark. "I'm taking it off."

"Then don't complain if paint drips on your head," Audrey said as she laughed. "I think you should wear it or you'll look even weirder with bright splotches of color in your hair!"

Mark grimaced, but he kept the rain hat on and it was a good thing because as they all worked on the huge canvas at the same time, paint was definitely dripping even though Shiloh was trying to be as careful as possible.

Desirae started to sing, "I'm painting in the rain, I'm painting in the rain," to the classic tune of *I'm singing in the rain*. Shiloh had forgotten what a beautiful voice she had. It brought back memories of when they had played in *The Legend of Sleepy Hollow* in the fall at the spooky Leroux Theater.

"Your voice! It is beautiful!" exclaimed Mrs. Dominguez. "Please keep singing so we can all hear."

Desirae said, "Thank you," and then she kicked up the volume a notch. The acoustics in the gymnasium were quite good and it made it seem like the class was painting the background scenery for a Broadway play.

Shiloh wished that Evan had been there. He knew that Evan loved Desirae's voice.

Right before the bell rang, Mrs. Dominguez said, "I'm giving extra credit to students who paint at lunchtime!"

Shiloh and Desirae looked at each other. They didn't have to say anything. They were both thinking that they would come back at lunchtime even though they didn't need the extra credit.

Chapter Five

The Pink Envelope

Wednesday evening Shiloh's dad picked him up from school, but before they went home, Shiloh had a question. "Dad, what do you think Evan would like for a gift? Desirae and I want to get him something and give it to him when he comes back to school."

"Hmmmm...." said his dad. "I don't know, but we have an hour or so before we have to get home so why don't we text your mom and tell her we're going on a shopping trip."

"Great! Thanks, Dad," said Shiloh. The local Target store was just a few miles from their house so Shiloh's dad drove there as he and Shiloh did some brainstorming about what Evan might like.

"Evan isn't into sports, but anything science, math, history, or art-related he really likes," said Shiloh.

"What about drama? He was pretty good in the *Sleepy Hollow* performance your class gave in the fall," said Shiloh's dad. "Not as good as you, but pretty close."

Shiloh laughed. "Well, you're kind of prejudiced when it comes to me."

"That I am, I confess," said his dad as he maneuvered the car into the Target parking lot.

Inside the store, they were wandering aimlessly for a while until Shiloh settled on the books, CDs, and toy area of the store. He wasn't really sure what he was looking for, but he knew that if he saw whatever the perfect gift was he would recognize it right away.

Finally his dad said, "Do you mind if I go over to the bedding section while we're here? Your mom has been complaining that her pillow is kind of lumpy so I was thinking I might buy some new ones."

"That's okay," said Shiloh. "I just hope I can find something for Evan."

"Take your time," said his dad. "We don't have to leave for 40 minutes or so. I'll come back over here so you don't have to scout around looking for me."

Shiloh had been looking in the toy and kit section for a little while when he noticed a girl who was looking at toys too. Something about her was familiar but he couldn't decide why. She was a little taller than the other girls he knew at Cornerstone so that made him wonder if she was older than he was. She was wearing a red jacket and red sneakers. Suddenly, she turned around and was looking at him. She waved at him. Then, she walked up to him.

"Hey, you're Shiloh right?" she asked. That was when Shiloh noticed that she had the most dazzling smile he'd ever seen. She had an unusual way of talking as if she were kissing and talking at the same time. Shiloh thought it might be a French accent but he wasn't sure.

"Yeah, I'm sorry, do I...do I know you?" he asked. He felt like the words wouldn't come out of his mouth.

"No," she said. "But I know who you are. You're Shasha's brother, aren't you?"

"Yep," said Shiloh, but as soon as the three-letter word was out of his mouth he wished he had thought of something more refined to say.

"My name is Gabrielle. I started at Cornerstone in January," she said. "I'm in some classes with Shasha. My family just moved here from the south of France."

"Oh, so you're in seventh grade?" Shiloh asked. Then he thought to himself—*that was stupid. Of course she's in seventh grade if she's in Shasha's class. And why didn't I say nice to meet you.*

"Yes. Your sister has been so nice to me. She really made me feel comfortable in class," said Gabrielle. "Schools in Europe are different. I was in sixth grade there, but when they tested me they put me in seventh grade here." She was looking directly into Shiloh's eyes as she talked and it was making him feel uncomfortable although he didn't know why. He noticed that she had light brown eyes with little specks of amber in them.

Shiloh didn't know what to say. He was wondering if she was his age or a little older, but he didn't ask.

"What are you looking for?" she asked.

For a second, Shiloh didn't know what she meant. He had completely forgotten that he was there looking for Evan's gift. "Looking for?" he mumbled. "Oh, yeah, a present...a present for my friend Evan."

"That's interesting. I'm looking for a present too," she said.

Shiloh didn't know what else to say, so he just stood there. He had the strangest feeling. He felt like there were things he wanted to say, but when he tried to get his mind around expressing the words, they just wouldn't come out. It was almost as if there were another Shiloh on the inside of him saying harsh things like, *don't say that or that's stupid or you don't know her well enough to say that.* Shiloh was usually so self-confident, but standing there near Gabrielle he felt more awkward than he ever had in his life.

Gabrielle stood next to him for a second and then she started to turn to walk away. Shiloh could smell lavender and vanilla. He wondered if it was a perfume she was wearing. "I've got to go now. Otherwise I won't find a gift for my friend," she said.

"Okay," said Shiloh. He shuffled his feet a little and stopped looking at Gabrielle. He pretended to be looking at the products on the shelf, but instead he was wondering why he felt so odd. He glanced sideways after she walked away and he noticed that she was picking up some boxes. He didn't want to make her feel uncomfortable by staring at her so he stopped looking over after a while.

A few minutes later, he looked up and she was gone. Then, he felt a little relief from the nervousness he had felt, but also sad to see that she had already left.

He walked over to where she had been standing. There on the shelf was a Thinking-Box kit for inventors. Gabrielle had picked it up and hadn't pushed it quite flush with the back of the shelf. *She touched this,* Shiloh could hear himself think. He brushed the thought aside because he realized he now had the perfect gift for Evan.

Just as he picked it up, his dad walked up carrying two huge, fluffy pillows. "Did you find something for Evan?" he asked.

"Look, Dad, it's perfect," said Shiloh as he held up the box.

"Wow," said his dad. "Evan's going to love it. Are you paying for it, or am I?"

"I don't think I have enough," said Shiloh. "Can I pay you back out of my allowance?"

"Sure, Kiddo, no prob," said his dad. "Ready to go?"

Shiloh nodded. They paid for their stuff and went to the car. When they got home, Shiloh was relieved that Evan's gift fit inside his backpack. He had completely forgotten how he was going to bring it to school in secret. He stuck it on his desk to bring to Cornerstone tomorrow.

He sent a text to Desirae.

```
Found a great gift
for Evan and bought
it to give from
both of us.It's a
Thinking-Box
Inventor's Kit.
```

Desirae wrote back right away.

```
Wow! That sounds
absolutely perfect!
We can wrap it at
the secret lab
tomorrow.
```

Later that evening Shiloh headed over to see Evan. When he got inside, Evan's mom said, "I don't think he's contagious anymore, but you better stay at least 10 feet away from him just to be sure. Your mom won't be happy with me if you catch Evan's cold. It was a doozy."

"Okay, Mrs. Smithfield, don't worry, I'll keep my distance," Shiloh said.

When he got into Evan's room, he was happy to see that Evan was up, dressed, and working at his computer.

"Hey, Evan! I almost expected to see you in your pajamas," said Shiloh.

Evan laughed and then he coughed into his arm. "No, I'm past the PJ stage," he said. "So glad to see you."

"I hope you're coming back to school soon. I think Cornerstone might cave in soon if you don't come back. All the teachers except for Sufferin have asked about you," said Shiloh.

At that comment, Evan perked up. "Did Desirae say that she missed me?"

"Yeah," said Shiloh, "and she gave me something to give to you."

"She did?" asked Evan. He was so excited.

Shiloh dug into his bag. He opened up the zippered pocket and pulled out the pink envelope from Desirae. He threw it across the bed like a

Frisbee so that Evan could pick it up on the other side of the room.

Evan picked up the envelope.

His hands were shaking a little. He opened it up. Inside was a folded over note with her initials DS for Desirae Stiles. Her cute cursive writing was on the inside.

Dear Evan,

Shiloh and I miss you so much!

We hope you get well soon.

Cornerstone isn't the same without you. We hope you're back in time for the Valentine's Day Dance.

Your friend,

Desirae

Evan sat down on the bed. He clearly seemed a little disappointed. Shiloh wasn't sure whether to ask about what Desirae had said. But, after a few seconds he went ahead and asked, "What did Desirae say?"

"I think she said that the both of you are a couple," said Evan.

"What?!" asked Shiloh. "I can't believe she said that! Where are you getting that idea? Desirae is just a friend."

"Well clearly SHE doesn't feel that way," said Evan.

Shiloh couldn't imagine what Desirae would have said that would make Evan think that way. The three of them were all close friends. *I mean sometimes I look at her and think...but still, we're just friends! I would never do that to Evan!*

"Here, read it yourself," Evan said as he flipped the folded note into the air.

Shiloh caught it and read it over twice. "There's nothing in this note that says that, Evan. It's a nice note that tells you how much she misses you. Maybe your head is just fuzzy, but I think you're being irrational."

"I'm being irrational? I'm never irrational!" Evan said as his voice went up in pitch. She says *Shiloh and I, we,* and *we,* that's three times! And she signs it *your friend.* I think that's pretty clear."

"You were definitely friend-zoned but not because of her and I. She just means that since she and I were at school and you weren't she said *we,*" said Shiloh. "Why would she mention the dance if she and I were a couple?"

"If she wanted to dance with me, she could have mentioned that," said Evan. He was starting to feel really depressed and his nose was getting clogged again.

"You're crazy," said Shiloh. "What did you expect? A passionate love letter?"

"A love letter would have been perfect. I guess I should just step out of this triangle so the two of you can get together. Shiloh, tell me the truth, do you like her?" asked Evan.

"Of course I do, but I don't like her in that way," said Shiloh, although he wasn't one hundred percent sure if that was true. "She's pretty and all, and she smells good...but I know you really like her so..."

"Maybe if I weren't clouding up the works with my huge crush on her, you'd try to get closer to her," said Evan. "Maybe, I'm the third wheel!"

"Now you're really talking crazy right now! You need to relax. We are all friends. Don't ruin it by saying something you'll regret," said Shiloh.

"Why does life have to be so complicated?" Evan asked although he didn't expect an answer. He seemed miserable.

"I think I'm gonna go home now," Shiloh said. He felt bad. He'd come over to lift Evan's spirits and the exact opposite had happened. "Oh, I almost forgot that Mrs. Dominguez asked me to tell you that you've got to get well soon because she says so," Shiloh said as he tried to smile. But Evan didn't notice. His visions of

being married to Desirae and their
future happy home with three
children were becoming dimmer and
he felt sad.

Chapter Six

My Funny Valentine

After school on Thursday, Shiloh headed down to the secret lab. He had been carrying Evan's gift with him all day in his backpack. Now he was worried that if he and Desirae took a picture to send to him that Evan would interpret this as part of the myth that he and Desirae were a couple. He was wracking his brain trying to come up with a way to explain this to Desirae without giving away Evan's secret crush on her.

When he got there, Desirae hadn't arrived yet. Shiloh opened up his backpack and took out Evan's gift. It made him think of his meeting with Gabrielle. Shasha had been so busy the past few days that he hadn't had time to ask her any questions about her new friend.

In a few minutes, he heard soft footsteps and Desirae came into the lab.

"Hey, Shiloh!" she said. "I can't wait to see the gift you bought for Evan. How much money do I owe you?" Shiloh looked up and as usual was relieved that it was her and not some interloper. He was always worried that one of the students, teachers, or the principal was going to find out about the secret lab.

"Well, my dad paid for it, but I owe him about $27 from my allowance now," said Shiloh.

"Wow! It looks worth it. It will take me a few weeks to pay you back. Is that okay?" Desirae asked.

"Sure," Shiloh said. He paused before he added, "I think it might be good if the gift came just from you, Desirae."

"What? Why?"

"I think that Evan feels a little left out since he's been out of school for so long.

I think the gift would mean more if it came just from you instead of from the both of us," Shiloh said.

"I don't understand," said Desirae.

"Well, when I brought him your note yesterday, I think he read a lot into the *Shiloh and I* part of it," said Shiloh.

"You mean he's jealous that I've been hanging out with you since he isn't here?" she asked.

"Well," said Shiloh. "He just seemed kind of sensitive about it."

"That's weird," said Desirae. "Maybe because he's been sick, he's feeling off or something. I thought you guys were best friends."

"We are," said Shiloh. "And I want to keep it that way, so let's just say the gift came from only you."

"Okay, if you think that's for the best. I can wrap it and send him a picture with a note from me, how's that?" Desirae asked.

"Great idea. That's perfect actually," said Shiloh. "While you're wrapping and sending him a text, I'll clean all these messy cobwebs up."

The two of them got to work. Shiloh found a broom and cleaned up all the hanging cobwebs, which wasn't easy without hitting the overhead lights and ducking the spiders that fell. Desirae turned on the radio and started wrapping Evan's gift with a plain red Christmas paper that could pass for Valentine's Day. Some romantic songs were playing and Shiloh was thinking that Evan wouldn't be happy if he knew the two of them were in the lab together. Desirae started singing along to the lyrics of *My Funny Valentine.*

When she was finished, she took a photo of the gift and sent it to Evan with this text:

> Please come back on Monday if not sooner!

```
This gift awaits
your return in the
secret lab.
```

In a few minutes, Evan sent back this text:

```
Is Shiloh in the
lab with you?
```

"Uh oh, Shiloh. Evan's asking if you're here with me," Desirae said.

"I think you should tell him *no,*" Shiloh said.

"This is dumb," she said. "I'm not going to lie."

"I know, I think so too. I don't know what's gotten into him. He was in kind of a bad mood last night when I went over to his house."

"Hmmmm...I don't like lying to him," she said. "But we don't want him to get upset. Just go outside the door so I can say you're not here."

Shiloh stepped just outside the lab door.

Desirae sent back a note:

> No, he's not here.
> I'm heading home in
> a few
> minutes. Just
> wanted you to know
> that I was thinking
> of you.

Evan sent back a note:

> I can't wait to get
> back. I love my
> mom's chicken soup,
> but there's only so
> much of it that I can
> eat!

Desirae gave Shiloh the all clear and he came back in.

"Evan sounds like he might be in a better mood today," Desirae said.

"That's good," said Shiloh as he dodged a large spider that fell off one of the cobwebs.

After half an hour had passed, Shiloh was finished with the cobwebs and the secret lab looked better.

"I miss the Christmas lights. I wish we could've left them up," said Desirae.

"Me too. I loved Santa's Workshop. Hey, Desirae, do you know a girl by the name of Gabrielle?" Shiloh asked.

"No, is she in sixth grade?"

"She's in seventh," Shiloh said, "but I think she's our age. She was in sixth grade in France but they placed her in seventh when she and her family moved here."

"I love that name. Gabrielle...it has such a beautiful sound and it seems so exotic," said Desirae.

"So does Desirae," Shiloh said without thinking. Evan wouldn't like it if he knew that he was complimenting Desirae. "They probably call her Gabby for short so it probably doesn't sound all that exotic," He tried to make a joke so that his compliment would be forgotten.

Desirae laughed. "Time for me to head out. My mom usually waits until I get home before she starts dinner. I usually help."

"I can walk you home if you want," Shiloh said. *Why did I say that? Evan is going to be so mad if she says yes.* Shiloh walked Desirae home so many times without any issues, but Evan was going crazy right now and he didn't want him to completely lose his mind.

"My dad's going to pick me up as soon as I text him, but thanks," she said.

Shiloh was relieved. "Okay. In that case I'll see if one of my parents can pick me up," Shiloh said. He texted his mom first and she wrote back to say that she'd be there in 15 minutes.

The two friends waited outside the school for their rides. Shiloh's mom showed up first. After they were on their way and Desirae couldn't see them anymore she started to walk home. She knew that neither one of her parents was available, but she had told Shiloh that her dad would be picking her up so he wouldn't insist on walking with her. She wanted to be alone with her thoughts and if Shiloh had walked her home, she wouldn't have had the quiet time she needed.

It was strange about Evan and Shiloh. She liked both of them a lot. Evan was super-smart and geeky. Desirae thought there was a good chance that he was as intelligent as Einstein. He was cute too in his own way.

Shiloh was funny and confident and cute too. He was more confident than Evan who seemed like he could jump out of his skin at any moment. Shiloh was easygoing, while Evan was always a ball of energy and filled with new ideas. Desirae thought that their opposite personalities was why they were such good friends.

Now if I could just meld them together they would make one perfect boyfriend, Desirae thought to herself and that brought a smile to her face. Shiloh's comments had made her wonder whether Evan had a crush on her. Did she have a crush on Evan? She wasn't sure. She certainly enjoyed being around Evan and had sensed that he sought her out more than Shiloh did.

***

The school week passed by quickly. Over the weekend, Shiloh and Desirae planned to meet up with both sixth grade and seventh grade kids from Mrs. Dominguez's other classes to help finish the painting of the canvases. Because she was an art teacher, Mrs. Dominguez was one of the few teachers who worked with more than one grade level. The students had all completed their backgrounds at this point and Mrs. Dominguez had given them four different themes, one for each canvas.

Their group was painting famous romantic couples of history. They had couples as diverse as Antony and Cleopatra and Mickey and

Minnie Mouse. It was a lot of fun for them to try to paint. Mrs. Dominguez was having them do sketches first, then transferring the sketches to the canvas with a transfer sheet, and finally painting in the details with fast-drying, acrylic paint.

When Shiloh got there on Saturday, he felt a different energy in the gym than he had before. He looked across and noticed that Gabrielle was there. He still hadn't had time to catch his sister when he could casually ask about her new friend. Seeing her again made Shiloh realize that he could have the beginnings of his first real crush. This was different than anything he had ever felt for another girl. Here and there he had feelings for Desirae, but Evan had quickly confided in him about his crush on Desirae so Shiloh had backed away.

Gabrielle noticed that he was there too. She talked to Mrs. Dominguez and then gracefully strode over to where Shiloh was standing. "Bonjour, Shiloh," she said as she smiled. Shiloh never knew what it meant when in novels it said, *her smile could light up a room.* But now he knew.

"Hey," Shiloh said. His inner voice was saying, *Can't you come up with anything better than that to say to her?*

"Is Shasha going to be here too?" Gabrielle asked. It was hard for Shiloh to concentrate on what she was saying. He was so distracted by her lavender and vanilla perfume.

"No...at least I don't think so..." said Shiloh as he stumbled on his words.

"Oh, that is too bad," said Gabrielle. "Your sister is talented, wouldn't you say?"

"Yeah...I guess so..." said Shiloh. *Why are you stumbling so much, she's going to think you're dumb,* he thought to himself.

"You mean you don't know?" Gabrielle asked. She was surprised that Shiloh wouldn't have an immediate positive response.

"No...I do know...yes, of course, you're right," said Shiloh. He realized that he was feeling anxious. It was a feeling that he didn't have often and it wasn't comfortable at all.

"Well, I must get back to my group," said Gabrielle.

"What is your group painting?" Shiloh asked. *Wow, that's the first halfway intelligent thing you've said to her,* Shiloh's inner voice said to himself.

"Mrs. Dominguez has us doing designs from vintage valentines," said Gabrielle. "I love her, but it's hard to understand her accent." Shiloh suppressed a smile at that remark since Gabrielle's French accent was just as strong as Mrs. Dominguez's Spanish accent. Then, Gabrielle paused and flashed a smile at Shiloh.

He stood there mute and watched her walk away. *Why didn't you think of something more fascinating to say?* His inner voice screamed at him.

Before he could think of anything else, Desirae wandered up to him. "Hey, Shiloh, who was that girl you were talking to?" Desirae asked.

"Hey, Desirae. That was one of my sister's friends. She just started at Cornerstone last month," said Shiloh.

"Oh," said Desirae. She noticed that Shiloh was acting weird but she didn't say anything. "Well, I'm off to paint a polka-dot dress on Minnie

Mouse. I heard from Evan this morning. He said he's feeling better and is coming back on Monday."

"That's good," said Shiloh. He was hoping that Evan wasn't still mad at him, but the fact that Evan had texted Desirae and not him said a lot.

Chapter Seven

Will You Be My Valentine?

Evan came back to school on Monday, but he still didn't feel like his normal self. Shiloh saw him briefly in the hallway and waved, but not only had he not received a text from Evan in more than three days, his wave back was weak and forced. Would their friendship be wrecked over the misunderstanding about Desirae? Shiloh was hoping that that wasn't the case.

It wasn't until Mrs. Dominguez's class that the three of them were able to talk. When Evan walked in, Mrs. Dominguez threw her arms up in the air with happiness. "Oh, thank goodness you are here, Mister Evan! This class is not the same without you," said Mrs. Dominguez. She wanted to hug him, but she restrained herself.

"I'm glad to be back too, Mrs. Dominguez," Evan said as he smiled.

"You are just in time for our next fun project!" she exclaimed.

Shiloh, Desirae, and Evan all sat close to each other, but the flow of talk among them wasn't as easy as usual. Desirae could feel the tension between the two friends, but she still wasn't a hundred percent sure what was causing it.

Mrs. Dominguez started the class. "Today, we are all going to start creating handmade valentines for our friends and loved ones. I am going to show you some paper cutting techniques and then you can use any of the supplies to create your own valentines. We have glue, we have stickers, we have glitter, and we have sequins! We also have paper doilies in different colors and construction paper! We have special pens for calligraphy too! I only ask that if you make a mess you clean it up so the next class won't have glitter all over their hands and clothes! We'll have four days to work on this project and of course you can continue to do this at home as well. Please check in with me if you want to take any supplies home."

"This is going to be so much fun!" said Desirae to Evan and Shiloh as she got up to get the supplies she wanted to use. "I have tons of valentines to make so I better get going!"

Evan was only thinking of one thing—*how was he going to make a valentine for Desirae if she was sitting right next to him?* He decided that the best thing to do was to make a bunch of different valentines, but not personalize them with messages until he was at home. That way Desirae wouldn't suspect that one of the valentines was for her.

Shiloh was wishing that he knew Gabrielle a little better. It didn't seem like a good idea to make a valentine for someone you had just met.

At the beginning of the class, there was a lot of conversation and activity as the students gathered their supplies, but as they started to work it got quiet. Mrs. Dominguez decided to play some romantic Valentine's Day music as they worked.

Shiloh wasn't paying much attention to the music until an old song came on. He couldn't really hear the lyrics except for the title, "Bewitched, Bothered, and Bewildered." That's when he realized it—he had a crush on Gabrielle and it wasn't a little crush. It was starting to become a big crush like the crush that Evan had on Desirae.

Just thinking about her made his cheeks flush. At that moment, Mrs. Dominguez walked by, "Are you okay, Mister Shiloh?" she asked. "I hope you are not getting the cold and the fever that Mister Evan had."

"I don't think so, Mrs. Dominguez," Shiloh said. He felt embarrassed and was so happy that no one could read his thoughts.

"It is a little warm," she said. "You know how it is in the winter. They set the heat too high and then we're roasting like peppers in here."

"I'm okay, Mrs. Dominguez, really," said Shiloh, but the truth was he wasn't feeling totally well.

After Mrs. Dominguez had walked past them, Desirae whispered, "Can we meet at you-know-where at lunch? Evan, I want you to open your gift."

"That sounds good," said Evan. Shiloh was going to say he could be there, but then he thought better of it. Maybe it would be a good idea to give Evan some alone time with Desirae.

"I can't make it," said Shiloh, but he didn't explain why and Desirae gave him a glare as if to say, *the gift is from you too!*

Class time went by quickly as the students worked on their valentines. Shiloh decided to make two, one for his mom because he knew she liked that kind of stuff and one for Gabrielle...he just wasn't sure if he would have the courage to actually give it to her.

At lunchtime, Shiloh went in search of Shasha, but when he saw her in the cafeteria, Gabrielle was already sitting with her and a group of Shasha's other friends. His questions about Gabrielle would have to wait. He should have known that it wasn't a good time, since Shasha was almost always surrounded by a group of her friends. She sometimes seemed like a rockstar with her fans.

Shiloh grabbed the standard school lunch tray and brought it over to a table where no one was sitting. The lunch of the day was pizza, which he normally loved, but he found that he wasn't as hungry as usual.

Valerie walked up to him. "Is it okay if I sit with you, Shiloh?" she asked.

"Sure," Shiloh said, but Valerie couldn't help but notice that he didn't sound too enthusiastic.

She sat down and then she smiled at him. "I can't wait for the dance on Thursday," she said.

Shiloh nodded as he took a small bite of his pizza. The pizza didn't seem to taste as good as usual. "Did they change the way they make this?" Shiloh asked.

"I don't think so," said Valerie. "It tastes the same as last week's. This is my favorite lunch. Maybe you're getting a cold. Sometimes that makes your taste buds dull out."

"I hope not," said Shiloh. "I hate being sick. Maybe you shouldn't sit here just in case."

"I'll go if you want me too, but I almost never catch colds," said Valerie. "I have a good immune system."

"I just wouldn't want you to get sick if I am," said Shiloh.

Valerie was facing out and she could see Shasha with her friends. "Isn't that your sister over there?" she asked.

"Yep," Shiloh said. He glanced over and noticed that Gabrielle appeared to be looking directly at him. He knocked over his knife and it hit the top of the table with a loud clang. Shiloh could feel the blood rushing to his cheeks.

"Shasha must be really popular. She always has a bunch of friends talking and laughing around her. I wish I could be like that," Valerie said wistfully.

"I think the key is to just be confident. I think you already are, you just have to believe in yourself," Shiloh said matter-of-factly.

"Are you always this deep?" Valerie was surprised.

"Not really, I just have a lot on my mind."

Shiloh and Valerie continued to chitchat over their bland pizza for the rest of lunch.

Meanwhile, back at the secret lab, Evan was opening up his gift. "I can't believe you got me something," said Evan.

Evan ripped open the paper with glee. Then, when he saw what it was, he was even more excited. "Desirae, this is great! It's got all sorts of odds and ends that I can use for my inventions. This was so thoughtful."

Before he could think about what he was doing, he reached out to give Desirae a hug. He held her for just a second too long and Desirae blushed.

"You know, the gift was really from Shiloh and me," said Desirae.

Evan put his hands down at his sides. "It was?" he asked.

"Yeah, I got the idea, but he's the one that picked out the gift," said Desirae. "We both missed you so much that we were trying to give you a boost so you'd come back to school quicker."

"Well, it worked," said Evan but he was thinking to himself, she said *WE* again. "I just hope I can catch up on all the stuff I missed." Evan was still annoyed thinking about all the time that Shiloh had spent alone with Desirae.

"While I was wrapping up your gift, Shiloh cleared all the cobwebs around here so the lab would be in good shape when you came back," said Desirae. "Shiloh's a really good friend."

"Yeah, I guess so," said Evan. He and Shiloh hadn't totally patched things up yet.

"Are you going to go to the Valentine's Day dance on Thursday night?" Desirae asked.

"Yes!" said Evan. "I wouldn't miss it if you're going to be there."

"I'll be there," said Desirae.

Finally, Evan blurted it out, "Are you going to dance with Shiloh?"

"Sure, I mean, I will, unless that bothers you," said Desirae.

"I was hoping we could dance all night together," said Evan. He couldn't believe he had gotten so bold that he said it out loud. He wanted to say, *will you be my valentine?* But he wasn't courageous enough for that and besides it sounded too syrupy.

"It's a school dance, Evan. I can't be rude if someone asks me to dance," said Desirae.

"Oh," said Evan. "I guess."

"We're not official or anything like that, Evan," said Desirae, "at least not yet."

Evan paid close attention to every word that Desirae said and when she said "at least not yet" it gave him a sliver of hope. It was enough for him to stay happy for the rest of the week.

Later that afternoon, when Shiloh got home from school he cornered Shasha in the kitchen.

"Hey, Shiloh. I feel like I haven't seen you in days," said Shasha. She was chewing on a celery stick with a small dab of peanut butter on it.

"Hey," said Shiloh. "I have a question for you. Do you think it's weird to give someone a valentine if you don't know them that well?"

Shasha laughed. "I did that a few times, but I just signed it *a secret admirer* so the person wouldn't know it was from me."

"Did they ever find out?" asked Shiloh.

"One of them did because they figured out it was my handwriting," said Shasha. "That was in fifth grade when I had a huge crush on this kid named Vic. He figured it out and then he made fun of me for the rest of the year."

"Do you still have a crush on him?" Shiloh asked.

"No, in fact I have no idea what I ever saw in him, but that's how crushes are," said Shasha. "What was I thinking? Yuck and double yuck."

"How many times have you had a crush on someone?" Shiloh asked.

"I don't know," said Shasha as she chomped on another piece of celery. "Maybe ten times."

"TEN times!" exclaimed Shiloh. "Wow! That's a lot."

"I used to hang up posters of some of the famous guys I had crushes on, but in sixth grade I took them all down," said Shasha.

Shiloh shook his head. "I don't understand women." He was going to ask Shasha about Gabrielle, but he didn't think he was ready to be subjected to Shasha's teasing once she figured out why he was asking.

Instead, he retreated into his room to think about Gabrielle without interruptions.

In a while, he came downstairs and set the valentine he had created for his mom on her cookbook stand in the kitchen.

He had decided not to sign it and had typed up the note he had written on the inside so his messy handwriting didn't ruin the card.

He had written the following:

I admire everything that you
do.
You bring grace and beauty
to ordinary, everyday tasks.
Our home is a loving place
because of you.

Later that evening, his mom came
into the kitchen to start dinner. She
saw the red envelope and opened it.
On the inside was a beautiful,
handmade valentine with small
glued-on sequins, glittery swirls, and
a red, lacy heart doily. After she read
the inside, a happy tear trickled
down her cheek.

Shiloh's dad walked in. He saw her
bent over at the cookbook stand.
"Are you okay, honey?" he asked.

"Thank you so much for the beautiful valentine, darling," she said as she turned toward him and kissed his cheek.

"Which valentine?"

"This one," she said as she handed it to him.

"Oh, that one," he said as he glanced at the text on the inside, "it expresses just how I feel."

Uh oh, he thought to himself. *I forgot all about Valentine's Day again. I wonder where this valentine came from?*

Chapter Eight

Shiloh's Secret Admirer

On Thursday morning, Shiloh was late to Sufferin's homeroom again. But, luck was on his side because Mr. Thomas was chatting with her in the hallway. Shiloh saw Mr. Thomas hand her an envelope. Shiloh wondered if Mr. Thomas was giving her a valentine. He still hadn't decided whether he would give the other valentine he had made to Gabrielle. He was so curious about her. There was something about her that was so different than the other girls at Cornerstone. Shasha would probably have said that Gabrielle was sophisticated. Maybe it was because she had lived in Europe.

At lunchtime, he and Evan and Desirae had decided to meet at the secret lab. Shiloh had been enlisted to pick up sandwiches for all of them and he had rushed off to the cafeteria to get them this makeshift picnic. The egg salad sandwich on whole wheat looked the best so he bought three of those, some potato chips, three cans of root beer, and three snack packages of cookies. His health-conscious dad would have disapproved.

When he got to the secret lab, Evan and Desirae were laughing and chatting away. *Good,* he thought to himself. *Maybe Evan and I can get back to where we were and not be at odds with each other.*

As he was unpacking the sandwiches, he noticed something unusual in his backpack. It was a rose-colored envelope. He pulled it out. He put the sandwiches and other food on their impromptu lunch table.

But before he could open the envelope and look at the contents, Evan said, "What's this?"

"It's egg salad," said Shiloh.

"Don't you remember that Desirae hates egg salad sandwiches?" asked Evan.

"No, sorry, Desirae, I forgot," said Shiloh distractedly. Evan was thinking to himself, *if Shiloh and Desirae were a couple he should have remembered that.*

"That's okay. It's only bad if the egg whites are super rubbery," she said. "I'll survive. What's that?"

"I think it's a valentine," said Shiloh.

"Oh, that's interesting. What does it say?" she asked.

"Maybe he doesn't want to tell us," said Evan.

"No, it's okay. I'll read it to you," said Shiloh, "it says...*I see the world through rose-colored glasses. Take my hand so you can see the world that way too...your secret admirer.*" Shiloh's cheeks turned red.

"Who do you think sent it?" asked Desirae. She seemed more than interested. "I love the decoration with the heart made of roses. It's beautifully drawn. It's very romantic."

"I don't know," said Shiloh as his cheeks got redder. "It's printed out with a computer font. There's no handwriting. Whoever it was must have snuck it into my backpack when I wasn't looking."

"Very mysterious," said Desirae, but she seemed to know more about it than she was telling.

"Did you send it?" Evan asked Desirae point blank.

"No, of course not," said Desirae. "I sign my valentines and I only made valentines for my family this year."

"Oh," said Evan. He was disappointed that he wasn't going to get a romantic valentine from Desirae because he had one for her. "Maybe we can pick up some clues if we think about it scientifically."

"That's a good idea," said Shiloh. He was happy to hear Evan in his science frame of mind again.

"It's way too romantic to be from a family member," said Evan, "so it can't be from your mom or your sister."

"The rose-colored glasses seem like a reference to the famous French song," said Desirae.

"Which song?" asked Shiloh. His heart was beating faster since he thought the valentine could be from Gabrielle.

"It's called La Vie en Rose," said Desirae. "I've never been to Paris, but that's the place I think of when I hear that song. I saw a photo of the Eiffel Tower with a perfect pink sky once. I'd love to go there someday."

Evan's mind wandered to an image of himself and Desirae on their honeymoon in Paris for a split second, but then he came back to reality. "The person who sent it must have a very upbeat view of life. That's what it means to see the world through rose-colored glasses. Do you know anyone like that?" asked Evan.

"Just about all the people I know are like that," said Shiloh, "except for Sufferin, and Evan at the moment." He nodded his head toward Evan.

"Hey!" Evan was shocked he was called out, but then he quieted down almost immediately as he remembered how he had been acting. He sheepishly grinned to try and break the tension.

"Does the valentine have any perfume scent? Sometimes girls like to do that--put a couple of drops of their perfume on love letters," said Desirae. Evan thought about how he would love to smell a letter with her strawberry scent.

Shiloh sniffed the envelope. He thought he smelled vanilla, but he wasn't sure so he didn't say anything. "This is silly," he said.

"Don't you want to know who it is?" asked Desirae.

"Definitely, but I still feel dumb sniffing something for perfume," said Shiloh.

"Do you know anyone who has rose-colored glasses or likes the color rose?" asked Evan. "That might be a clue."

"Roxy loves that rose color," said Desirae. "She wears it all the time. Haven't you noticed?"

"No," both Evan and Shiloh said at the same time.

"Whoever it was is very skilled at art," said Evan. "The drawings of the roses are perfect. Of course, they could have had someone else create it for them if they didn't create it during class time."

"Maybe Mrs. Dominguez meant to give it to her husband and it dropped into my backpack instead," said Shiloh. That made Desirae and Evan laugh.

"But you're bringing up a good point, Shiloh. The valentine might

have been given to you by mistake,"
said Evan.

"I never even thought of that," said
Desirae. "That's actually possible."
Evan was listening to Desirae
closely. There was something in the
sound of her voice that made him
think that she knew who it was and
had been sworn to secrecy.

Suddenly, Shiloh got a ping on his
phone. It was his dad.

> Hey son, did you make
> a valentine for your
> mom?

"It's my dad," said Shiloh.

"Is everything okay?" Desirae asked.

"Yeah, he's just asking me if I made
a valentine for my mom," Shiloh
said.

"Did you?" said Desirae.

"Yes," said Shiloh, then he sent a
text back.

```
Yes, I thought
she'd like it.
She has the other
ones I gave her.
```

His dad wrote back.

```
She thinks it was
from me, so don't
tell her! I'll
break it to her
when I get the
right moment.
```

Shiloh turned to his friends. "My mom thought the valentine I left for her was from my dad and he didn't tell her that it wasn't."

"Uh oh," said Evan, "sounds like there's going to be some drama at your house. You didn't sign it?"

"No, I thought for sure she would know it was from me since it was handmade," said Shiloh. "I used to make handmade valentines for her when I was little."

"Well, we better get out of here," said Desirae. "It's time to get back to class."

"How was your sandwich, Desirae?" asked Shiloh.

"Rubbery, but not too bad," said Desirae.

"Just five more hours and it's dance time," said Evan. "I'm so glad I feel better today."

The Valentine's Day dance was scheduled to start at 7:00 pm. The gym had been cleaned up and the mood was festive. The canvases that they had painted were the perfect backdrop for photos of couples and friends. The boys and girls had adhered to the dress code. The boys looked handsome in their suits and ties and the girls looked lovely and very grown-up in their party dresses.

The school had sprung for a real band and they were playing all kinds of music.

Shiloh was paying attention to every clue Desirae and Evan had brought up to see if he could figure out who had placed the valentine in his backpack.

Desirae looked stunning in a copper-colored dress that highlighted her hair. She had piled it up in a bun on her head and had placed tiny roses in her curls.

"Wow! Desirae, you look beautiful," said Evan. "Will you dance the first dance with me?"

"Of course, Evan. You look wonderful," she said as she reached out to straighten his wayward tie.

Shiloh smiled as he watched them slow-dancing on the dance floor.

Some of the teachers were dancing too. Mrs. Dominguez was dancing with her round, jovial-looking husband. Ms. Sufferin had on an even uglier black dress, but Mr. Thomas didn't seem to mind as he danced with her, well sort of. It wasn't quite dancing when there was only one person moving and the other one waving a ruler in the air, pointing it at different people who walked by.

"Shiloh, can I have this dance?"

Shiloh glanced over to see Roxy standing there. She was wearing a frilly, rose-colored dress.

"Sure," said Shiloh. He whisked her out on the floor, but she quickly stepped on his feet.

"Oh, Shiloh. I'm so sorry. I really want to dance with you, but I'm not very graceful," she said tremulously.

"No worries," said Shiloh. "My clodhoppers, as Ms. Sufferin calls them, will survive.
Can I ask you something?"

"Sure," said Roxy.

"Have you ever written a valentine and signed it as a secret admirer?" asked Shiloh. He watched Roxy's face to see if she would show any expression that would give him a clue.

"No," said Roxy. "I've written out lots of valentines, but I'm always too shy to give them. In fact, the guy I like the best doesn't even know it."

Shiloh was about to respond, when Valerie walked up. "When the music changes, I want the next dance," she said to Shiloh as she swirled away in her full-length blue dress.

"I see that I have competition," said Roxy.

Shiloh just smiled, but he felt embarrassed. He was trying not to let all the attention go to his head.

The next dance was a fast dance, but Valerie grabbed his hand and practically pulled him out on the dance floor. She was a very good dancer, but she was quite a bit shorter than Shiloh, so he found himself hunching over like a misshapen scarecrow in order to talk with her. After screaming a question or two he determined that she hadn't given him the valentine either.

The secret admirer field was beginning to narrow and then from across the room, he saw Gabrielle. She was wearing a shiny green party dress. She looked gorgeous. His palms started to get sweaty and his feet seemed twice their normal size.

She had been talking to the band and had asked them to play a special song.

She walked gracefully across the gym floor and went straight to Shiloh. Shiloh was feeling so nervous.

"Shiloh, can I have this dance?" she asked.

"Yes...sure...of course," said Shiloh as he stumbled on the words. He had wiped his sweaty palms on the inside of his jacket pockets so that Gabrielle wouldn't notice. The music started to play *La Vie en Rose* and they were slow dancing.

"This is one of my favorite songs," she said as she quietly sang the words in French close to Shiloh's ear.

For a few minutes, it seemed like he and Gabrielle were the only ones on the dance floor. Shiloh wondered how difficult it would be to learn to speak French.

He thought for sure that the valentine must be from her, but he could hardly believe it. He never asked her any questions to find out. He decided that he would give her the valentine that he'd made in class.

But, from the sidelines, Audrey was watching them dance. She had a huge crush on Shiloh and had told Desirae in secret. She had given Desirae the valentine and asked her to put it in his bookbag. She had drawn the beautiful heart of roses by hand.

Other girls might have been upset watching Shiloh and Gabrielle dance, but Audrey was too positive to get moody. She saw the world through rose-colored glasses and was determined to win Shiloh's heart.

And as for Evan and Desirae, they danced every dance together and at the end of the evening Evan gave her a special valentine. It was an evening that neither of them would ever forget.

Shiloh's dad finally admitted to Shiloh's mom that he hadn't written the valentine, but she just laughed and said she was play acting and knew it all along. She was hoping he'd feel guilty and bring her some flowers and take her out to dinner, which was exactly what he ended up doing. She put the beautiful valentine from Shiloh in her scrapbook with the others that he had made for her years before.

Acknowledgments

I want to thank my family again for their support. Your continual affirmation and encouragement is what keeps me going. I love you.

About the Author

Rita Onyx is a member of the Onyx Family who also include Mirthell, Shalom, Sinead, Shasha, and Shiloh. Together they have a successful social media and YouTube following with over 1 million subscribers and over 1 billion views across their channels. Check out Onyx Family, Onyx Kids, Onyx Life, Playonyx, and Cardionyx on Onyx Flix, YouTube, Prime Video, Facebook, Instagram, Twitter, and Amazon to find their new videos, books, and merchandise. You can also hear Rita Onyx along with the family on The Onyx Life Podcast.

Other Onyx Kids Books:

Getting to Know Onyx Kids

Onyx Kids Shiloh's School Dayz #1 –
The Sealed Locker

Onyx Kids Shiloh's School Dayz #2–
The Class Pet Fraud

Onyx Kids Shiloh's School Dayz #3 –
The Phantom of the School Play

Onyx Kids Shiloh's School Dayz #4 –
The Secret Santa

Made in the USA
Columbia, SC
21 April 2020

93116445R00076